Balzer + Bray is an imprint of HarperCollins Publishers.
Snow Much Fun!

Library of Congress Control Number: 2018964818
ISBN 978-0-06-274112-7

The artist used a mix of handmade props and photography to create the illustrations for this book.
Typography by Dana Fritts
19 20 21 22 23 SCP 10 9 8 7 6 5 4 3 2 1
❖
First Edition

For Alessandra,
a friend for all seasons
—N.S.

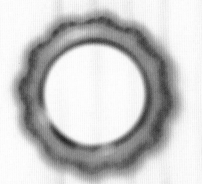

For Jacob
and Samuel
—S.G.

Bear Facts

Snow Much Fun!

By NANCY SISCOE

Illustrated by SABINA GIBSON

BALZER + BRAY
An Imprint of HarperCollins Publishers

Berry was the first to see.

"Oh! Snow!"

"I am SNOW
ready for snow!"

"Snow?"

It snowed and it snowed
through a day and a night,

until everything in sight
was covered in white.

Two of the friends were ready to go,
but Willow was moving a little bit slow.

"I've got the sled!"   "I've got the skates!"

"I've got . . . marshmallows."

"Willow?! Don't you want to go out in the snow?"

"Um . . . no?"

"But snow is my absolute favorite thing. C'mon, let's go!"

First they went sledding.
They squooshed on together.
Berry gave a push–

"Eeeeeee!"

"Wheeee!"

Then whoosh,
shoosh,
smoosh!

Willow brushed herself off
and laughed and then . . .
they ran up the hill to do it again.

Back home by the fire,
the friends warmed their toes.

"That was SNOW
much fun!"

"I know something
even better. . . ."

"Promise that it won't be wetter?"

Skating was Berry's favorite thing.
Out on the ice, Berry was twirling and whirling.

Ginger was gliding and sliding.
Willow was flopping and plopping.

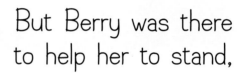

But Berry was there
to help her to stand,

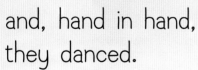

and, hand in hand,
they danced.

"That was nice
on ice!"   "Tomorrow let's go–"
                    "Anyone for cocoa?"

Ginger loved to build.
First they rolled and molded.
Then they packed and stacked.

And soon they had made a whole
parade of snow bears and snow hares.

Two frosted friends searched high and low.

"Where'd Willow go?"

All the snowballs they'd been making
had reminded her of baking. . . .

"Snowball cookies, anyone?"

"Oh yes!"

"Oh yum!"

The next morning it was storming,
but Willow knew what they could do.
And by the time all the popcorn and apples
were strung, the storm was done.

"It's for the birds,
not for you!"   "But I'm hungry too."

Next they strapped on some skis

and hung their garlands
from fences and trees.

The new snow was shimmering
as the friends went skim-skimmering
down powdery hills, till thrills
turned to chills.

The cocoa was gone and the fire was dying
when Willow said, a little bit shy,

"There's a game I've been
wanting to try. . . ."

They cleared off the ice and set up some nets

for the slip-slidingest game of hockey played yet.

Willow gave a quick flick of her stick—

"She shoots! She scores!"

"Goooooaaaaaaaall!"

Willow had found a new favorite thing!
Though—who knew what tomorrow might bring?

"Where'd she go?"

"Look—out the window . . ."

A winter full of flurries had only begun.
And three furry friends will have SNOW much fun.